TIMMY'S SEARCH

Materials for Christian Education
Prepared at the Direction of General Convention

TIMMY'S SEARCH

By Harry Behn

Illustrated by Barbara Cooney

THE SEABURY PRESS

Greenwich, Connecticut

THE SEABURY SERIES is prepared for Christian education in parishes and missions by the National Council of the Protestant Episcopal Church in the United States of America at the direction of the General Convention.

THE REV. DAVID R. HUNTER, Ed.D.
Director
Department of Christian Education

THE REV. LESTER W. McMANIS, M.A.
Executive Secretary
Division of Curriculum Development

© *1958 by The Seabury Press, Incorporated*
LIBRARY OF CONGRESS CATALOGUE CARD NUMBER: 58-9260
271-760-HK-40-15
Second Printing, 1960

When Timmy was safe and snug in bed
As any planted seed, he said,
"If God would tell me, I would know
Just where He lives, and I would go
To Him who made the birds that sing,
The flowers that grow, and everything,

And I would thank Him for the shade,
The bees, and rustling leaves He made
So different in shape and size,
And for the stars, and then sunrise,
And food, and everything He gives—
If I could find out where He lives."

THE GARDEN

Just before Timmy fell asleep, he heard crickets chirping in the garden. It was a peaceful, comfortable sound. They were saying over and over how happy they were in their homes under the leaves in the moonlight. Timmy was as comfortable and happy as a cricket. But he was wondering about something.

Timmy was wondering if God's home might be somewhere in his own garden. But he wasn't sure. A year ago—the spring before this one—he had looked and listened everywhere. He had seen and heard what anyone sees and hears in gardens in

7

springtime. But he had not quite discovered God, and he wanted to. He fell asleep thinking that tomorrow he would look and listen more carefully. It was the evening of Timmy's sixth birthday.

The next morning turned out to be the first really warm day of spring. You could almost see new leaves stretching to grow. Robins were standing stiff on the lawn, listening for worms. A bluebird flew by, pink and blue, like a flower, looking for a place to build a nest. Somewhere among the blossoms of the apple tree a phoebe called, close, but sounding far away. And along the wall, daffodils were beginning to open as wide as Timmy's eyes and ears.

Old Jim was out back somewhere, clinking his trowel on a flowerpot. Old Jim was much too busy to need any help, so Timmy climbed up in his apple tree and looked out at the world. He looked over the wide field that spread far away and gradually became a wood. He was wondering what it was he had planned last night to look for.

Timothy Baxter Brown had never been to school. He had never been to kindergarten. Or to

Sunday school. He had hardly ever been any place except downtown a few times with his mother to have his hair cut. But next fall he was going to go to the first grade because at last he was six years old.

Every morning two children went by outside his fence on their way to school. In the afternoon they came by again on their way home. They were bigger than Timmy. Their names were Gretchen and Walter Tubbs.

Gretchen liked Timmy. Walter did, too. He was younger than Gretchen but almost as tall.

Sometimes Walter acted up, but he could be very nice when he wanted to be.

On Saturdays nobody much went by. On Sundays, Walter and Gretchen went by on their way to Sunday school. On their way home they talked to Timmy through the fence about all kinds of things. Sometimes they talked about God.

But sometimes Walter sang a song about Timothy Baxter Brown and laughed.

When Walter sang, Gretchen would look ashamed of her brother. She never said anything because one time she did and it only made him sing louder. When Walter sang, Timmy would climb up in his apple tree and wait until they had gone. He didn't like Walter's singing, but it *was* funny.

This first warm day of spring nobody went by because it was Saturday. Old Jim was too busy to need any help. So Timmy watched the robins, and listened to the phoebe, and tried to remember what it was he was going to discover.

He remembered a long time ago when all there was in the world was his yellow Teddy bear. And a window so sunny it made him sleepy. That was when he was a baby.

He remembered when he was older, and his father used to rake all day in the garden. And the day his father broke the rake and went downtown to buy a new one. When he came home he was smiling because he had a job selling things in the hardware store.

After that, an old man named Old Jim came to live in the fixed-up half of the woodshed and dug up all the plants Timmy's daddy had planted and planted them in different places.

Old Jim didn't answer questions right away. He liked to think things over. Timmy didn't mind. He liked to think things over, too.

This morning he was trying to think what it was he had decided to discover. He couldn't seem to remember, so he looked at his birthday present.

On the outside this birthday present was like a watch. Only it didn't tick. It was a compass. On the inside it had one hand that floated and always pointed to the mountains beyond the end of Farm Road. That was north. The other end pointed to a pine tree in Miss Reese's yard. That was south.

Those two directions never changed.

Beyond the stone wall, over a field and a woods where the sun came up, was east.

West was downtown, but all you could see that way was Mr. Elder's big barn. Unless you went out in the middle of Virginia Street, which Timmy never did because he was not allowed to.

The more Timmy looked at his compass, the more he wondered what it was pointing to in those mountains beyond the end of Farm Road. He went out back to see if Old Jim might know.

Old Jim took plenty of time to think it over. He sat down on his wheelbarrow and took off his gloves and pulled a splinter out of his finger.

While Old Jim was thinking, suddenly Timmy remembered! He remembered what he had planned last night to discover!

"I know what my compass is pointing to," he said. "To God!"

"Yep," said Old Jim.

Somehow Timmy was disappointed. Those mountains seemed so far away.

"Mebbe you didn't notice," said Old Jim, "that a compass needle has two ends. Mebbe both ends of it point to Him."

Timmy looked to the north. Then he turned around and looked to the south.

"Mebbe each end of it points to God," said Old Jim.

"How could it?" asked Timmy.

"Mebbe each end of it points to each of his great gentle hands holding the world between them."

Timmy looked slowly across the sky, from the pine tree in Miss Reese's yard to the mountains beyond the end of Farm Road. "God must be pretty big," he whispered.

"He is," said Old Jim, and went back to work.

Timmy looked at the sky where a few small
white clouds were floating. Everything in the
whole beautiful world seemed very peaceful.

He climbed up in his tree and sat there. When
the wind fell still, he heard the sawmill humming
over near Tillot's Grove.

15

He had never been to Tillot's Grove, but he knew it was there, beyond the wide field and the creek you couldn't see but could sometimes hear. He had never been to school, but he knew there was one, and he was going to go to it. He had never seen God, but now he knew—God held the world gently between His hands, the whole world with all its flowers and trees and singing birds.

Timmy thought it was only polite to say thank you to God for all these wonderful things. So he did.

LISTENING

Timmy looked and looked up through the apple blossoms at the sky. He was listening to hear if God said anything. But all the sounds were on the earth. A dove calling, far away. Children playing a game. And Old Jim clinking flowerpots. That was all.

Suddenly a white puff like a feather drifted up over the trees near Tillot's Grove. It was steam from the twelve o'clock whistle blowing on the sawmill. Timmy hung by his hands on a branch, let go, and landed on the ground. Even then he had to wait before he heard the toot of the whistle.

17

It took that long for the sound to come drifting over from the sawmill.

Old Jim stopped clinking flowerpots and began making other sounds, gathering up his tools. He never worked after noon on Saturdays. When the weather was nice, he sat in his old wicker chair outside his woodshed and thought about things, and smoked his pipe, and talked to Timmy.

When the noon whistle had finished blowing, Timmy went over to the woodshed and sat down against it in the shade. Old Jim was inside washing up. Timmy made a scratch along the ground at the edge of the shade, and watched the sunshine slowly drifting across it. When Old Jim came out and sat down in his chair, Timmy made another scratch along the new edge of the shade and asked, "How long does it take when God says something for it to drift down out of the sky?"

Old Jim took a longer time than usual to think this over. He closed his eyes. When he opened them again and looked at Timmy, he said, "Where's that compass of yours?"

Timmy took the compass out of his pocket. The needle still pointed to the same two directions.

Old Jim didn't take the compass. He turned his head and listened to something. "Do your hear a dog barking?" he asked.

Timmy listened, and said he did, a long way away.

"What direction do you hear it from?"

Timmy looked at his compass, and pointed south.

"Futher away than Miss Reese's pine tree?"

"Oh yes," said Timmy, "a whole lot farther."

"Didn't you tell me the south end of your compass points to that pine tree?"

"I did," said Timmy, "and it does. But—"

"What did I say it pointed to?"

"To one of God's hands."

Old Jim took plenty of time to light his pipe before he said, "What both of us told each other was make-believe, Timmy. That needle doesn't point just to any mountain or pine tree, or any other one thing you can see or hear. Whatever I said, God doesn't live only up in the sky or any other one place. The truth is, He lives everyplace, forever." Old Jim was thinking very carefully.

So was Timmy.

He was thinking about everyplace, and forever. They both seemed farther away than the mountains beyond the end of Farm Road. Much too far away to hear anything from. "Then I guess nobody can hear God," he said.

"Yes they can. Everybody can hear Him—if they listen. You try."

Timmy tried listening. He didn't hear anything special. Only an airplane. And some carpenters pounding and sawing. It was no use. "How *do* you listen everyplace at once, Old Jim?"

"Inside yourself."

Timmy laughed. "How can I when my ears are outside myself!"

"Try again," said Old Jim.

Timmy tried again, and thought of something. "Is it like remembering?" he asked.

"Yep," said Old Jim. "And a mite like wondering why."

"Why what?" asked Timmy.

Old Jim didn't answer this. He asked another question.

"You like being Timmy, don't you?"

"Yes. Yes, I do."

"Why? Don't you ever wonder why?"

"I never did before," said Timmy. "Why *do* I like being me?"

"Because God made you, Timmy, and loves you. That's why. You think about it."

So Timmy thought. He thought about God living everyplace, forever, making everything and everybody, and still having time to remember about one little boy named Timothy Baxter Brown who lived at 529 Virginia Street. It was wonderful.

Timmy was so busy thinking about how wonderful this was that he hardly heard Old Jim say, "That's what I mean by listening."

It was like remembering everyplace, forever.

Then he thought of something else. Where he was, right there in his own garden, exactly where he stood, was a part of everyplace. That is how Timmy knew that God *did* live in his garden. And was probably right that minute noticing what a nice day it was.

Timmy looked up at the sky where an airplane went buzzing along like a big slow bee. Now he knew that God wasn't just up there. Now he knew that God was everyplace, and it didn't seem far away at all. He listened and heard doves calling, and airplanes humming, and carpenters sawing, and dogs barking, and children laughing and shouting everywhere!

Then he heard his mother calling, and he and Old Jim went in to lunch. They were both good and hungry.

BELLS AND PEOPLE

THE best thing about Sunday morning was the bells. They weren't like the alarm clock bell that made Timmy's father jump up and eat his breakfast and hurry to the hardware store. Sunday bells made Mr. Brown go back sounder asleep, even with the sun already shining in the morning sky.

Timmy's mother fixed breakfast for just the two of them, and they had a nice visit, talking quietly so they wouldn't waken Daddy. After breakfast, Timmy went outside to wait for Gretchen and Walter Tubbs to come by on their way to church.

Sunday bells floated and hummed in the sun. They rippled away, and came back booming and singing. They weren't like school bells that worried about children being tardy. They weren't like fire alarm bells that got so excited they could hardly ring. Or the ice-cream man's thirsty little bell. Or cowbells that wandered over the hills. Sunday bells called out to people all over the world, saying: How peaceful it is! How peaceful it is to go to church! How peaceful!

Every other day of the week, people worried about where they had to be in a few minutes. Sometimes even the milkman and the postman and the man who took away the garbage hardly noticed when you said Hello.

On Sunday, though, people were different, as different as Sunday bells.

There was Miss Reese, who was so deaf she could only smile. It was a happy smile that told you she knew where she was going and there was plenty of time.

And there was Mr. Elder. Every Sunday he opened the squeaky doors to his big barn and drove his car out and picked up Mrs. Elder at their front gate. It was the only day they ever drove their car. Mr. Elder was a lawyer. All week he worked hard trying to make people be fair to each other. That's what he said, and he seemed pretty cross about it. Only on his way to church he was quite cheerful.

There was Captain Dewitt who drove by so fast on weekdays nobody knew what he was like. The only day he didn't drive was on Sunday. Then you could see that he was very fat and as slow a walker as he was a fast driver. Timmy always called Hello to him, and he always called back, Hello Son. He wasn't Timmy's father, of course, but that is what he always said. Son. Timmy's real father said that Captain Dewitt was a tired corporal who kept books for the Water Company.

Then there was Mr. Hightower who rode a bicycle and wore glasses. He was Walter's Sunday school teacher who sold toothpaste on weekdays in Hightower's Drugstore. One time, after his haircut, Timmy went there with his mother for a root beer, and Mr. Hightower gave him a free sample of a candy bar. Everybody liked Mr. Hightower

because he was always happy. Gretchen said he could sing like a bird. But Walter thought he sounded more like a frog. Walter liked frogs.

Sunday people were certainly the most different from each other. Even Mr. Jameson and his three boys. They were farmers. They all had red hair, but that was the only way they were alike. One day Timmy said Hello to them. Mr. Jameson didn't even turn around. His boys did, though. One of them looked sad. The next one smiled. And the last one winked. After that, every Sunday when they walked by in a row, they each did exactly the same thing.

Walter said the Jamesons didn't have a mother

or a car. They did have a big truck, but they never drove it to church. Timmy didn't know their first names.

His favorite friends, of course, were Gretchen and Walter. Especially Gretchen. Sometimes Walter could be nice, too, but this morning he was terrible. He was so terrible that Gretchen came walking ahead of him pretending he wasn't there. Walter was jumping around looking in old weeds for dried cockleburs. When he found one he stuck it in his hair. Then he jumped around Gretchen and tried to make her notice him. But she wouldn't.

"What's he being, an Indian?" asked Timmy.

Gretchen shook her head.

"I'm being the devil, that's what," said Walter. He sat down where a lilac bush leaned over both sides of the fence, like a shady cave. This was where they always visited.

Walter didn't *look* bad. He never sulked. He almost always smiled. It was only when he began to laugh that you had to watch out. Now he was only smiling, so Timmy thought he was over being bad, and asked Gretchen, "Why was he being the devil?"

"Because," she said, and turned away.

Walter laughed. "I'll tell you why, Mister Timothy Baxter Brown! Because Gretchen was scared to ask you something."

Timmy looked at Gretchen and asked, "What?"

"Something I didn't think was very polite," she said.

Walter didn't care if it was polite or not. He went right ahead and asked Timmy, "Why don't your parents ever let you go outside your yard?"

Gretchen looked at her brother severely, but it

was not really a cross look. "I told you, Walter. Because Timmy is only six."

"When I was six I went everyplace," said Walter. "I still do. Any place I want to. After school. Until the five o'clock whistle."

"Parents are different that's all," said Gretchen. "Besides, maybe Timmy does go everyplace he wants to."

"*Do* you?" asked Walter.

Timmy nodded.

"Then why don't you go to church?"

Timmy couldn't think what to say.

Walter laughed, and shouted to Gretchen, "I told you so! His mother and father won't let him go!" He began to pull cockleburs out of his own hair and stick them in Gretchen's.

She didn't pay any attention to him, and threw the burs out in the street. Walter jumped over to get them, but he forgot about the burs when he found some ants dragging a dead wasp.

Gretchen smiled at Timmy, and said, "Walter's acting this way because our parents make him go to Sunday school. They send him so they can get

a little peace and quiet. Sometimes it makes him even worse."

"Ouch!" said Walter. An ant had stung him on the leg. He scratched the bite, and began running around and buzzing. He said he was being the dead wasp going to heaven.

"Wasps don't go to heaven, do they?" whispered Timmy to Gretchen.

"I don't think so. I do know God made people like Himself. People can live in heaven. I don't know about other things."

Timmy's eyes opened wide. "Are we like Him?" Gretchen nodded.

"How are we?" asked Timmy.

"Well, God can decide anything He wants to. When He made us, He decided to let us decide some things ourselves. We can even decide to be bad if we want to."

Timmy didn't think this was very sensible. "I think He ought to just make everybody good all the time. Why doesn't He?"

Gretchen wasn't sure. "I guess He doesn't *force* us to do things His way," she said, "because He wants us to love Him only because we want to."

This seemed like a good reason to Timmy. It was very polite of God to let people do things because they wanted to.

"Why *do* people do bad things?" he asked.

Gretchen didn't know. "Maybe because they're lonely. They don't realize that when you love God you can't be lonely. Are you ever lonely, Timmy?" she asked.

He shook his head.

"Neither am I, really," she said. "But sometimes my mother and father are."

Timmy hadn't thought about it before, but now he guessed maybe his mother and father were lonely, too. Lots of times he noticed that they sat all Sunday afternoon on the porch swing together and didn't say anything at all to each other. It seemed to Timmy as if they were remembering something sad that had happened a long time ago. All at once he didn't seem to know them very well. They were kind, and they loved him very much. But he was sure they were lonely.

"At church," he asked Gretchen, "do people find out how God wants them to be?"

"Yes," she said.

The bells began to ring again, and Gretchen jumped up. Walter was still buzzing and yelling that they'd be late. She ran along the sidewalk while Timmy ran along inside the fence, hopping over the flower beds. When he came to the corner, Gretchen said she was sorry, but she had to hurry to quiet Walter so he wouldn't act up when they got to Sunday school.

After Gretchen had quieted Walter and they had disappeared over the top of Virginia Street, the bells stopped booming and humming and drifted away until the only sound in the sunny air was the calling of a dove.

Timmy went back and sat under the lilac bush. For a long time he thought about God letting everybody make up his own mind. Of course, God wanted everybody to be good. He had so much to do, He certainly didn't want everything upset everywhere, forever.

To Timmy, it seemed easy enough to be good. All you had to do was do what you knew would make God happy.

Maybe Walter would discover this sometime. But if Walter did decide to behave himself, Timmy hoped he wouldn't be *too* good. Because Walter was quite nice the way he was, when he wasn't being terrible. Anyway, Walter and Gretchen were Timmy's best friends. Especially Gretchen.

LONELINESS

TIMMY was sitting up in his apple tree thinking how easy it was to be good on such a beautiful day with white clouds watching at the edge of the sky. Watching and listening. Sometimes it would be warm and still. Nothing would move at all. Then little twisting puffs of wind from nowhere would spin away over the lawn and shake petals off the apple tree.

Timmy hung on a branch and dropped to the ground. In a few minutes he was very busy exploring different places to see what he could find.

Sure enough, he found something. Out where

Old Jim dug up ashes to put around the rose bushes he found an old piece of iron shaped like a big bird's claw. It was rusty. He washed it off under the faucet. Then he walked by the wood-shed to see if he could ask Old Jim what it was.

He peeked in the door and saw that he couldn't ask right then because Old Jim was wearing his glasses. That was about the only rule Old Jim had. When his glasses were on, Timmy wasn't to bother him about anything. So Timmy didn't. He didn't say a word.

After a while Old Jim heard him standing there and looked out over the top of his glasses. He took his glasses off, and looked at the rusty piece of iron, and said, "That happens to be a foot off of some-body's old stove." Then he began to read again.

Timmy walked over to the stone wall and put his new discovery in a tin can on a flat rock where he kept things he found. His best treasures were a brass button with an anchor on it and several pieces of broken dishes with painting on them. But his very best, his father thought, was an Indian arrowhead, and very old.

Once upon a time these things belonged to people who had disappeared. Timmy hoped they had all gone to heaven. If they hadn't, he thought, how lonely they must be, just being noplace.

He heard a soft humming inside the house. It was his father's electric razor. Someday, he supposed, somebody would dig that up, too, broken and rusty under the dirt, and wonder who had shaved with it. Nobody would know it was his father.

All at once, Timmy felt very lonely.

He went up on the porch and sat on the steps and began to remember what Gretchen had told him. She said people who love God just couldn't be lonely. But Timmy was.

Maybe there was something else about feeling this way that Gretchen hadn't told him. Maybe when anybody was lonely, everybody was. Maybe when somebody was sad, or bad, so was everybody else, a little. Maybe all you could do was try harder to be happy and good. That might make everybody a little less lonely.

Timmy knew that his mother and father were

lonely. He wondered why. He listened and heard
his father go into the kitchen, and sing a little, and
talk pleasantly to his mother. They didn't sound
lonely. But Timmy knew that *somebody* was.

Then he saw something that surprised him.

It was too early for anybody to come home from church, but out on the sidewalk, watching through the pickets, was Walter, and he wasn't laughing, or even smiling.

Timmy went over to the fence and stood looking at Walter, and Walter stood looking at him. Timmy had never seen Walter this way before, not jumping around or up to something, but very quiet.

"Did they send you home?" asked Timmy.

"No," said Walter, "I came by my own self."

"Why?"

"Because."

"Because why?"

Walter turned away and said, "Because Mr. Hightower told us a story I didn't like."

"What did he tell you?"

"Never you mind what. It isn't so!" Walter gave the fence a kick and began to walk away. Then he turned around. He was crying. "God is *not* dead!" he said angrily.

Timmy couldn't believe anyone would say such

a thing. "Is that what Mr. Hightower said?" he asked.

Walter took hold of a picket and began to twist it. "He said some people killed God, that's what he said!"

Timmy thought this was a terrible thing to say. It couldn't be true, of course. There wouldn't be any world! And there was. A bright, dancing world full of sunshine and wind!

Walter was looking out across the wide field. When he turned around he seemed more like himself. He almost smiled. "There's a pond over at Tillot's Grove," he said. "I think I'll go over there and catch me some pollywogs." He noticed Timmy's tin can on the flat rock by the wall and asked, "Will you lend me that tin can, Timmy, to carry my pollywogs in?"

Timmy went over and emptied his things out of the tin can and gave it to Walter.

When Walter took the can he said, "Don't you tell Gretchen where I went! Do you promise?"

Timmy didn't want to say yes. But he was sorry for Walter, so he nodded. That was the same as saying yes.

Walter thumped on the tin can like a drum and walked away as if he didn't care about anybody or anything. He didn't go down Farm Road where his house was. He went straight across the wide windy field toward the woods and the sawmill and Tillot's Grove.

Timmy climbed up and sat on the front gatepost. His lonely feeling was still there. It was worse than ever.

The wind began to blow more and more and the sun shined brighter and brighter. Then Gretchen came running down Virginia Street with her hair blowing across her face.

Timmy jumped off the gatepost and waited for her.

"Did you see Walter?" she asked all out of breath.

Timmy said, "Yes."

She looked across the field with its tufts of grass and bushes swirling in the wind. "Did he go over to Tillot's Grove?"

Timmy didn't say a thing.

Gretchen stood looking across the field and asked again, "Did he?"

Timmy said, "No."

This wasn't true. But he had promised Walter not to say. He felt very cross and asked Gretchen, "Why would Mr. Hightower tell Walter something that isn't so!"

Gretchen sat down on the sidewalk. Quietly she asked, "What did Mr. Hightower tell Walter?"

"That God is dead!"

Gretchen sighed. "Walter should have listened more carefully. He should have waited to hear the whole story. The wonderful part that happened *after* He died."

"What did happen?" asked Timmy.

"He rose from the dead and went back to heaven where He lives forever and ever."

Timmy was glad.

Suddenly Gretchen jumped up and ran down Farm Road toward her house to see how Walter was.

Timmy sat on the grass for a long time. He was glad to hear what Gretchen had told him. But he was sad, too, because he had told her a lie.

Even if Timmy had promised Walter not to tell, he shouldn't have lied to Gretchen. He only did because Walter was scared, and lonely. It was too bad Walter hadn't listened more carefully to the whole story.

After a while, Timmy said to God, "I'm sorry I told Gretchen what I did. And would You please explain to Walter that You *are* alive and all right so he'll feel better?"

Timmy went over to arrange his things on the flat stone by the wall. He wasn't lonely any more, just sad. He stacked up his pieces of painted dishes, and thought about God.

That was when Timmy decided to ask his parents to let him go to Sunday school.

REASONS

TIMMY's mother had a rule for herself. She never actually said no to anything Timmy asked. When he asked for something she didn't approve of, her rule was to suggest something else more interesting.

When Timmy asked if he could go to Sunday school, she didn't say no. She simply thought what fun it would be if next Sunday she and Daddy and Timmy all went for a picnic together over to Tillot's Grove. "Wouldn't that be exciting?" she asked.

"Yes," said Timmy, slowly.

Mrs. Brown could see that they would have to ask Daddy about Sunday school after all. And this worried her.

She and Timmy were sitting on the porch swing. Old Jim was sitting in his chair outside the wood-shed softly blowing tunes on his harmonica. Mr. Brown was taking a nap.

Timmy imagined going over to Tillot's Grove for a picnic. He thought he would take along a new tin can and catch pollywogs and watch them turn into frogs. He might even see the sawmill close, and the whistle that puffed up white steam. It *was* exciting to imagine.

But he wanted just as much to know more about God and His whole wonderful world. That was exciting, too.

He had never exactly promised God about going to Sunday school. He couldn't do that without his parents' permission. But he certainly hoped they would let him go.

His mother was holding his hand.

"Don't you want me to go?" asked Timmy.

"Yes," she said, "I do. *I* would like all of us to go to church together every Sunday."

"But Daddy doesn't want to?"

"No."

"Why doesn't he?"

She laughed at Timmy and hugged him. "Let's both pray for him to want us to."

"Praying is like asking God, isn't it?" said Timmy.

"Yes. One kind of praying is asking with all our hearts. Let's pray for Daddy to believe the way he used to, so he'll know that God is not cruel, but kind." She closed her eyes for a minute and then whispered, "Amen."

"What does 'amen' mean?"

"That we mean very, very much what we say."

Timmy could feel how lonely his mother was. "Why does Daddy believe God is cruel?" he asked.

And so she told him. "Before you were born, we had a baby girl. She was very sweet. And very happy. Her name was Alexandra Louise. We loved her very much."

"Did she used to play in this yard?"

"No, dear. In those days we lived in a big city."

Timmy guessed what had happened. His mother's voice sounded far away. "One day our baby girl ran into the street and was hit by a car."

While his mother was thinking, Timmy watched a bumblebee bumbling against the porch ceiling. Then he looked out at Virginia Street crinkling in the hot sunshine. He understood several things now, better than he had before. Why his parents were so careful about making him stay inside the yard. And why they were lonely.

· His mother took his hand again. "That night, we didn't know if our baby girl would live. We prayed for God to let her live. But she died. Daddy thought that wasn't fair."

Timmy guessed that his mother would like to be quiet for a while, so he went out and climbed up in his apple tree and spoke to God.

"God," he said, "will You please explain to my daddy that You are taking care of his little girl so he will decide You are his friend again, and let me go to Sunday school. With Walter and Gretchen.

Then will You please tell my daddy to take my mother and me over to Tillot's Grove in the afternoon for a picnic. So I could catch some pollywogs and watch them turn into frogs. Amen."

WALTER'S SONG

THE next morning was Monday. The first bell had already rung when Gretchen came by going to school, but without Walter. She walked on the other side of Virginia Street, slowly, and kept watching for Timmy.

He jumped down out of his tree and called to her through the fence, "Gretchen, why are you walking over on that side?"

She didn't say anything.

"Are you mad at me?" he called.

"No, Timmy," she said, and he knew she wasn't. She came across the street and sat down on the sidewalk.

He felt ashamed about what he had told her. "I said what I said, Gretchen, because Walter made me promise."

"I know."

Then Timmy asked, "Where *is* Walter?"

Gretchen whispered, "He's hiding somewhere. When I go on to school, he's going to jump out and sing a song. Just don't pay any attention."

"What's he going to sing about? Me?" whispered Timmy.

"Yes. And when he does, don't you go and climb up in your tree, because that's what he's going to sing about. My daddy helped him with the words to this one. My daddy thinks Walter's funny." She looked around for her brother, and called him a few times. But he didn't answer. "He'll hide where he is all day if I don't go."

"Gretchen?" Timmy said.

"Yes?"

"Did you tell Walter the end of the story?"
She nodded.

"Did he feel any better?"

"He pretended it didn't matter. But it does. Lots more matters to Walter than he lets on."

When she had gone, sure enough, along came
Walter. He had been hiding around the corner
of the wall. He was laughing, but he sounded all
stuffed up and croaky. "I caught a terrible cold,"
he croaked, proudly. "Yesterday I fell in the pond
and nearly drownded. Now I sound like old Mr.
Hightower. My father says maybe I swallowed a
frog." He laughed again and began to cough.

"Aren't you going to sing your song?" asked
Timmy.

Walter seemed surprised. "What song?"

"The one your father had to help you with the
words of."

"Oh, that one," said Walter. He snuffled a little, and sang the song. There wasn't much tune

because he had such a sore throat. This is what he sang:

> "Mister Timothy Baxter Brown
> Climbed a tree and never came down.
> Is he a bird or a bat or a bee?
> He's up too high for me to see.
> Do you suppose when he is old
> He'll still be up there, good as gold?"

"That's a nice song," said Timmy.

"Nice!" croaked Walter. "It's supposed to be funny."

"It is," smiled Timmy.

"Then why don't you laugh?"

So Timmy laughed. He really did. Because it *was* funny.

Walter looked disappointed. "Why don't you go and climb up in your old tree?"

"I will," said Timmy, "after you go to school."

Walter looked as mean as he could. It wasn't a *very* mean look, because he didn't have much practice looking that way. He almost always smiled.

So this look was only a sort of snuffly, stuffed-up face.

"I'm sorry you caught a cold," said Timmy.

"Oh, it isn't so much of a one," snuffled Walter, and sneezed.

The tardy bell rang, and Walter ran up Virginia Street as fast as he could.

Timmy thought about Walter's father. About how he didn't seem to worry even when his little boy fell in a pond.

Timmy felt sorry for Walter. But sort of proud of him, too. Because Walter was never the least bit sorry for himself.

RIPPLES

THE next day was a happy one for everybody. It wasn't only the lovely weather, with a good smell of cut grass when Old Jim mowed the lawn, or the whirring of the lawnmower, or the butterflies fluttering. The nicest part was that people noticed all these wonderful things. Even the postman stopped to look and sniff the sweetness and smile.

All morning, Timmy's mother sang one song after another, and baked a batch of cookies with almonds.

When Mr. Brown came home for lunch, even before the noon whistle blew on the sawmill, he was carrying an ice-cold watermelon. Mrs. Brown smiled and scolded him because it must have cost a fortune so early. But she was pleased.

So was Timmy.

His father smiled. He had brought another present for Timmy, something in a small carton that went *peep peep*. It was a real, live, yellow baby duck that peeped and snuggled in his hands when he held it. The little creature looked at him with one bright, black eye and then the other and said, "Peep, peep, peep!" So Timmy named him Peeper, and they all laughed. Old Jim put him in a box with a screen over it while they went in for lunch.

While they were eating lunch, Timmy's father

talked about some new machinery they were starting to sell at the hardware store, and how much he was beginning to enjoy working there. One thing he said was very funny. He said when he was bringing home the watermelon it got heavier and heavier and colder and colder. He said he nearly decided to turn around and go back downtown and buy a car to carry it home in. The only reason he didn't, he said, was because he was already more than halfway home and it would have been farther to go back than to keep going. Mrs. Brown laughed.

At last it was time to cut the watermelon. It had light green and dark green stripes. When it crackled open, it was a beautiful red with smooth black seeds. Timmy had the first taste. It was sweet and ice-cold and juicy.

Timmy and Old Jim took theirs out on the back steps where they could spit out the seeds.

After a while, Timmy's daddy came out and sat with them on the steps. He was very happy.

Timmy put the empty rind of his watermelon in the garbage can, and hopped across the lawn. Close

to where the sprinkler made a wet circle, he got down and crawled on his stomach near enough for the falling drops to wash the sticky off his hands.

His father was talking pleasantly to Old Jim, and asked him if he knew Mr. Jameson, the farmer who had three boys.

Old Jim did, and thought Mr. Jameson was a good citizen.

"I'm about to sell him a new tractor," said Mr. Brown. "He's promised to let me know some time this week." He got up and called good-by into the house and went out the gate to go back to the hardware store.

Timmy ran across the yard, jumping over the flower beds. He was waiting at the corner before his father got there on the sidewalk outside.

When his father stopped, and looked at him, and smiled, Timmy didn't know what to say, except, "I'm glad."

His father was a little puzzled. "What about?" Then he ruffled Timmy's hair and laughed, "Your little yellow duck? And the watermelon?"

"Yes," said Timmy. But it wasn't only his little

yellow duck and the watermelon he was glad about. He was glad his father didn't seem the least bit lonely any more. And he thought he knew why.

All the rest of the week was the same. *Everybody* seemed happy. "Why do *you* think they are?" Timmy asked Old Jim. "Because my daddy has made friends with God?"

"Could be," said Old Jim. "Anyway, he's happy. And being happy is like when you toss an acorn onto a still pond. Ripples spread out and out, and every drifting leaf begins to dance."

"A pond like over at Tillot's Grove?" asked Timmy.

"Or any place," said Old Jim.

Timmy pretended he was a ripple, and rolled across the lawn to wash his hands and face in the cool drops from the sprinkler.

Old Jim let Peeper out of his box, and the happy little duck followed Timmy, waddling and running and falling down over nothing and getting up and running again. Peeper was so interested in everything you could hardly believe he

was only one week old. "Only a week ago," Old Jim said, "he was still inside his shell."

Timmy held the snuggly little duck close to his ear and listened to him chirping while he thought about two things. One was going for a picnic over at Tillot's Grove. Before he caught any pollywogs, he would throw an acorn on the pond and watch the ripples. The other thing he was thinking about was going to church. With his father and mother.

After a while Peeper got sleepy, and Timmy put him back in his box. Then he stood still in the spray of the sprinkler where a piece of rainbow shined and disappeared and shined again.

He was pretty wet by this time, but he didn't mind. He was thinking about next Sunday and how pleased Gretchen was going to be. And how surprised Walter was going to be.

Walter was already over his cold, and up to things as usual. But all the other children at school had colds. Colds were like that, Gretchen said, and measles. They spread. Like ripples on a pond.

For a minute Timmy didn't feel quite so sure about next Sunday. Suppose *he* caught Walter's cold and had to stay in bed all day and couldn't go to church?

Or even worse. Suppose some other ripples happened before Sunday and made his father change back again to being lonely?

Timmy knew this was just being afraid. Sometimes bad things did happen. Especially when you turned away from God and didn't trust Him. But Timmy trusted God very much.

He did feel chilly, though, and went in the

house to take off his wet shirt. His mother gave
him a dry one, and he put it on.

While he was buttoning his buttons, he asked,
"May I please have two empty tin cans?"

"Of course," she said. "But whatever for?"

"One to keep my things in that I discover in the
yard."

"And the other?"

Timmy was looking out of the window, watching Old Jim spraying a bush.

Again his mother asked, "What's the other can for?"

"Oh," said Timmy, "to bring home something I might happen to catch. If we happen to go for a picnic sometime."

His mother laughed, and found him two new shiny tin cans with no sharp edges and with lids.

SUNDAY MORNING

WHAT happened on Sunday Timmy just couldn't believe. Everything disappointing, and lonely, and sad. And then, at last, something more wonderful than anything that had ever happened before!

When he woke up he knew it was an important day. The night before, when he was almost asleep, his mother had told him she was perfectly sure they were all going to church together. Daddy had looked a little sad. He had said, "You know how I feel." But he hadn't said no. That was when he was being a little cross anyway about Mr. Jameson not coming in yet to buy a tractor.

When Timmy got up, he noticed that his

mother and father weren't simply up and dressed, they were dressed up. He guessed why. But he didn't say anything. He just ate his cereal, and hummed to himself, and waited for them to tell him that they were all going to church together.

All at once, his mother started to cry.

Timmy looked at her. Then he looked at his father, and asked, "Aren't you going to church?"

"Yes," said his father.

"Then why is Mummy crying?"

His father looked ashamed and said to Timmy, "Your mother and I are going to church."

Timmy began to feel that something was awfully wrong. "But not me?"

His father shook his head. "I'm sorry," he said.

"Not even to Sunday school with Walter and Gretchen?" asked the little boy.

Mr. Brown began to be angry, and said to Mrs. Brown, "You know very well I don't want to be upset having to worry about Timmy going any-where with those strange children, having to cross streets, and getting home safely. I don't want to have anything on my mind except business!"

"What business?" asked Timmy.

His mother explained. "Mr. Jameson told Daddy he would come to the hardware store and decide about buying a tractor. But he didn't come. So Daddy decided that when Mr. Jameson walks by on his way to church, we'll go out and walk with him."

"This is very important," said Mr. Brown. "Important to all of us. And I want to know that Timmy is safe here in his own yard with Old Jim."

"Old Jim," said Mrs. Brown, "was counting on going to church, too."

"Nonsense!" said Mr. Brown.

Then Mrs. Brown really began to cry.

Timmy couldn't say anything.

He went out and sat down by Peeper's cage and let him peck his finger. Big tears kept wetting his face, and he couldn't stop them. His father was going to church all right. But not for any reason except to sell Mr. Jameson a tractor.

What Timmy had wanted was for his father to stop being angry at God. But now his father

wasn't even angry. He wasn't anything. He just
didn't care.

"All right then," said Timmy, "neither do I.
I don't care about Peeper. Or Old Jim. I don't
care if my father and mother go to church and
leave me home and sell Mr. Jameson a tractor
or not. I don't care about anything."

He went over and sat under the lilac bush
and waited for Gretchen and Walter to come by.
He kept saying he didn't care if they did or not.
But he began to feel worse when they didn't.

He kept saying he didn't care, and kept kicking
the wobbly fence picket that Walter had almost
twisted loose. He kicked until the picket came
off and fell outside on the sidewalk.

Then the Sunday bells began to ring. And
Timmy began to cry harder than ever. The more
he cried, the worse he felt, until he said he hated
the bells, and his father, and his mother, and Old
Jim, and his new little yellow duck.

That was when he decided what *he* was going
to do. He was going over to Tillot's Grove and

catch a whole canful of pollywogs because he didn't care.

He took one of his new tin cans, and crawled out through the hole in the fence, and walked across the wide field with the early morning sun shining unpleasantly in his face.

About that time, Old Jim came out of his woodshed dressed up in a very clean black suit. He looked at the house. Then he gave Peeper a fresh pan of water.

When Mr. Jameson and his three boys came

walking up Farm Road, Mr. and Mrs. Brown walked out on the porch.

Old Jim asked Mr. Brown, "Where's Timmy?"

Mr. Brown was watching the Jamesons coming along in a row. He said to Old Jim, "Timmy's staying here with you."

"Where is he?" asked Old Jim.

Mrs. Brown looked around the yard and said, "I thought he was out here."

"Nope," said Old Jim. "I haven't seen him since breakfast."

Mrs. Brown ran back into the house.

Mr. Brown was thinking about something else. He stood on the porch and watched Mr. Jameson coming along. He watched Mr. Jameson and his three boys walk by and not even notice him.

Mrs. Brown came out of the house and looked around the yard, and up in the apple tree, and out back.

Mr. Brown didn't pay any attention to what she was rushing around about. He walked down the steps and said, "We're all dressed up, so we might as well go to church anyway."

Mrs. Brown wasn't thinking about going to church. She was thinking about Timmy, and she was scared.

Mr. Brown saw how white her face was. When she said, "Timmy's gone," he forgot about selling Mr. Jameson a tractor. He was afraid. And ashamed.

Old Jim wasn't afraid. He saw the hole in the fence where a picket was missing. He noticed that one of Timmy's new tin cans wasn't on the flat stone where it had been. He didn't mention these things. He simply told Mr. Brown to go and look down by the Tubbs's house while he looked someplace else.

Mr. Brown hurried out the gate and ran down Farm Road.

Old Jim smiled at Mrs. Brown, a smile that said there wasn't anything to worry about. She sat on the porch swing and waited.

When Old Jim went out across the wide field, he was still smiling as if he was glad all this had happened. As if he knew that something much better was going to happen very soon.

THE DEEP WOODS

OLD Jim walked out across the wide field. When he got into the middle of it, he saw that it wasn't a field at all, the way it seemed from town. The grass stood in big tufts wide apart and very high. The ground in between was bare and dry, with little animal trails going every which way. It was a lonely place where a small boy might easily get lost.

But the wide field wasn't as lonely as the creek you couldn't see but could sometimes hear after

77

a rain. Now it was dry. It was only a scattering of rocks winding away along the earth.

Beyond these dry rocks, trees began, a few at first, then more and more until they made a deep, dark, shadowy forest. Tillot's Grove and the sawmill were somewhere in this forest.

Before Old Jim went on among the trees, he stopped, and looked back. The bare, dry place where he stood was higher than town. He could see over the top of Virginia Street all the way down to the First National Bank building, and the grammar school, and the stores. In the bright sun of that Sunday morning, everything was very still.

Old Jim was thinking carefully. He knew how Timmy must have felt, finding out that his parents were going to church without him. Old Jim knew how any little boy would feel, coming out here alone for the first time. For a while he wouldn't notice much where he was.

But about here, Old Jim guessed, Timmy would begin to feel the loneliness. He would want to turn around and look back. He would wonder how his house looked from so far away. He would begin to hope that someone had missed him and was coming out to find him and take him home.

But Timmy wouldn't look back, not yet. He would hold on tight to his loneliness. He would go on across the rocks in the dry creek. He would throw away his tin can. Yes, there it was, shining among the rocks.

Old Jim knew where Timmy *would* stop, where he would turn around and look back, and start to think again. That was when he came to the edge of the deep woods. He would suddenly discover that he was alone. He would notice that all the time he had been walking away, he hadn't been going toward anything at all.

But then he would remember again how unfair his daddy had been. He would say he didn't care, and go on into the forest no matter how big and dark and scary it was.

Old Jim was right. That is exactly what Timmy did.

The tremendous trees and the leafy, shadowy

stillness scared him a whole lot more than Old
Jim knew. Still, he kept going on and on, deeper
and deeper into the woods, until he was lost.

Every way he turned seemed to be the way he
had come from. He was really lost, and he knew it.

Then, the strangest thing happened. He wasn't

afraid any more. He looked around at the trees and vines and wild flowers, and the great, piled-up, mossy rocks and patches of ferns. He smelled the cool, damp smell, and listened to softly whispering leaves. He climbed up on a big old crumbly log covered with moss and ferns, and

sat there, very small and still in the tremendous
stillness, and listened. And what he heard seemed
to him to be God's voice, soft and gentle, as it

82

said, "Timothy Baxter Brown, who lives at 529
Virginia Street, I'm sorry you didn't understand
that I was working things out for you. I'm sorry

you had to behave like this. I couldn't shake your daddy into being my friend, could I? I couldn't shove him into church, could I? But he *was* going this morning, wasn't he?"

"Yes," said Timmy, feeling very ashamed and small in the stillness.

"You didn't like his reason, that's all. Well, it was a kind of small human reason. To sell Mr. Jameson a tractor. But look at it another way. Why did your daddy want so much to sell that tractor?"

"I don't know."

"Then try to imagine."

So Timmy guessed, "To get some money?"

"That's right. Can you guess why he wanted that money?"

"No."

"Because he wanted to buy a car so your family could go for picnics together, and visit around a little, and make some friends in the town. Because he loves you and your mother very much, that's why. And I don't call that a completely bad reason."

Tears came into Timmy's eyes, and he said, "I'm sorry I didn't understand. I hope You'll forgive me."

"I forgive you," said the voice of the deepest, most peaceful stillness in the world. "Now don't you worry about it any more. But, Timmy, will you please try to remember that what *you* might want, even a kind, good thing, can't always be arranged in a minute. Try to be patient with Me. I'm patient with you, as well as everybody else in the world. Will you try?"

"Yes," said Timmy. "I'll try never, never to turn away from You again!"

The tremendous, quiet voice sighed. "It's no fun when you do, is it? For either of us."

Timmy shook his head.

He was wondering if God would help him find his way home again.

He took the compass out of his pocket and looked at it. The needle floated the way it always did. Only it wasn't right at all. It pointed to east and west! But Timmy kept his wits about him. He turned the bottom of the compass around

until the needle pointed to north and south. Then
he thought very carefully.

He knew he had walked away from his house
toward east. Now, if he walked west he would go
out of the deep woods into the wide field. From
there he could see his house and run home. So
he started to walk through the woods in the direction of west.

He stopped. That way didn't feel right. It felt
like exactly the wrong way. He thought again,

and discovered the trouble. He was holding the compass the wrong way. Slowly, he turned the compass around until north was where south had been. Then west was in the direction that felt right, and that was the way he started to go.

In the cool shadows of the deep wood, Timmy knew that God was helping him.

Just then someone said, "Hello, Timmy." And there was Old Jim standing on a high mossy rock among the trees, smiling, and puffing on his pipe. "Seems you got lost," he said.

"I did," said Timmy. "But I'm not lost any more." As fast as a squirrel, he climbed up to the top of the high rock and took hold of Old Jim's hand.

PROCESSION

Mr. Brown was pretty worried when he got to the Tubbs's house and asked if Timmy had come down there.

"No, Mr. Brown," said Mr. Tubbs, "I haven't seen your little boy. Walter and Gretchen have told me about him, though. They say he likes to sit up in trees."

Mr. Brown noticed Mr. Tubbs's funny smile, and he didn't like it. He said, "I thank you for your information," and started to go.

Walter, who was listening inside the screen door, came out and said, "I bet I know where Timmy went."

"Where?" asked Mr. Brown.

"To church. I bet he waited for me and Gretchen to come by, and when we didn't he went there by himself."

Mr. Brown thought this was probably so, and felt a little less worried.

Then Walter said, "The reason Gretchen and I didn't go when we usually do was because we're going to church at eleven o'clock—with our father and mother!"

Mr. Tubbs finished tying his necktie. "Seems funny," he said to Mr. Brown, "that a boy like yours should care so much about going to church. Or did he just get tired of being shut up in his yard?"

Mr. Brown felt his face turning red.

Walter went inside his house, and for once didn't slam the screen door.

Mr. Tubbs came down off his porch. "Do you know what I heard, Mr. Brown?" he said. "It may not be true, but I heard that you told the old man who works in your garden you'd fire him if he ever went to church."

"That's not true!" said Mr. Brown, angrily.

"That's what people think."

"I don't care what they think!"

"Yes you do," said Mr. Tubbs quietly. "I'm not too good a Christian myself. But I am beginning to *want* to be. Walter and Gretchen have taught me something. That Sunday can mean more than sitting around lazy and lonely reading the paper. It's beginning to dawn on me that this world is only the way families are. Well, the Tubbs family has about decided to change a little and do a few things together."

Mr. Brown couldn't say anything.

Then Mr. Tubbs asked in a more friendly way, "What business are you in, Mr. Brown?"

"Hardware," said Mr. Brown.

"That so?" said Mr. Tubbs. "I sell insurance."

"That so?" said Mr. Brown.

"Do you like selling hardware?" asked Mr. Tubbs.

"Well," said Mr. Brown, "I'm beginning to like it better than I thought I would. It's a job. I like tools and machinery."

Mr. Tubbs looked sad. Sadder than he really felt.

"The way I feel about insurance, it's not what I like best. But it's a job. What do *you* like best, Mr. Brown?"

"Music," said Mr. Brown before he really thought. But it was true. "I used to like to play the piano."

"That's funny," said Mr. Tubbs. "What *I* like better than anything else is to play the piano. And write songs. Mostly funny songs because I guess what's in my head is mostly feathers. But my children like to hear them, especially Walter."

"That so?" said Mr. Brown, and started to go again.

"Have you got a piano?" asked Mr. Tubbs.

"No," said Mr. Brown.

"Well, I have," said Mr. Tubbs, "and if you ever want to play it, you're welcome."

Mr. Brown didn't say anything, so Mr. Tubbs went back up the steps.

"Mr. Tubbs?" said Mr. Brown.

"Yes?"

"Thank you very much."

"Oh, that's all right. How about a concert this afternoon?"

"This afternoon," said Mr. Brown, "Timmy and Mrs. Brown and I are hiking over to Tillot's Grove for a picnic. Why don't we all go together? Both our families."

"Why not?" smiled Mr. Tubbs. "We can talk about it at church. O.K.?"

Mr. Brown thought for a minute. Then he smiled, and said, "O.K."

On his way back home, Mr. Brown was surprised to find he wasn't worried about Timmy any more. He felt that something wonderful had happened. To him, and to Timmy, and the world. He knew what it was, of course. Now he believed again, in people, and himself, and in God's goodness and love.

He was almost across Virginia Street when Mrs. Brown came running out of the gate and pointed across the wide field. There was Old Jim, taking his time, as usual, with Timmy walking along beside him.

Mr. Brown was surprised. He had been so sure that Timmy had gone to the church.

Timmy ran up to his father. He stood looking at the ground, ashamed because he had gone out of his yard without permission.

"I'm sorry," he said.

Mr. Brown knew what Timmy was thinking. "Get yourself washed up," he said. "We're going to church. Together. With our friends, Mr. and Mrs. Tubbs and Walter and Gretchen."

"And Old Jim?" asked Timmy.

"Of course," smiled Mr. Brown.

While Timmy was washing up, Mr. and Mrs. Brown sat on the porch swing. He held her hand and said, "You've been very patient with me."

She held his hand, tight, and looked down, and said, softly, "God, for Thy goodness and love, and for Thy Son, Jesus Christ, I thank Thee."

And Mr. Brown said, "Amen."

It was a happy procession that marched up Virginia Street that Sunday. Mr. Brown and Mr. Tubbs, Mrs. Brown and Mrs. Tubbs, Old Jim and Walter, and Timmy and Gretchen.

Walter looked up at Old Jim and asked, "Do you *like* being a gardener?"

"Yep," said Old Jim.

"Then that's what I'm going to be when I grow up," said Walter and turned a handspring.

The Sunday bells were ringing, humming and booming peacefully in the spring sunshine. Gretchen and Timmy thought the bells sounded like trumpets and harps and choirs of angels.